MERMAIDS

CYNTHIA HEINRICHS

with *illustrations by* JUMIN LEE

All day I sit in the classroom and look out at the water. All day I wait for school to end so I can go down to the sea to watch the mermaids. My mother is a mermaid and every day she dives in the sea with her flock of mermaids. They bring up abalone and seaweed, octopus and sea urchin, and all kinds of shellfish. All day long they dive and dive.

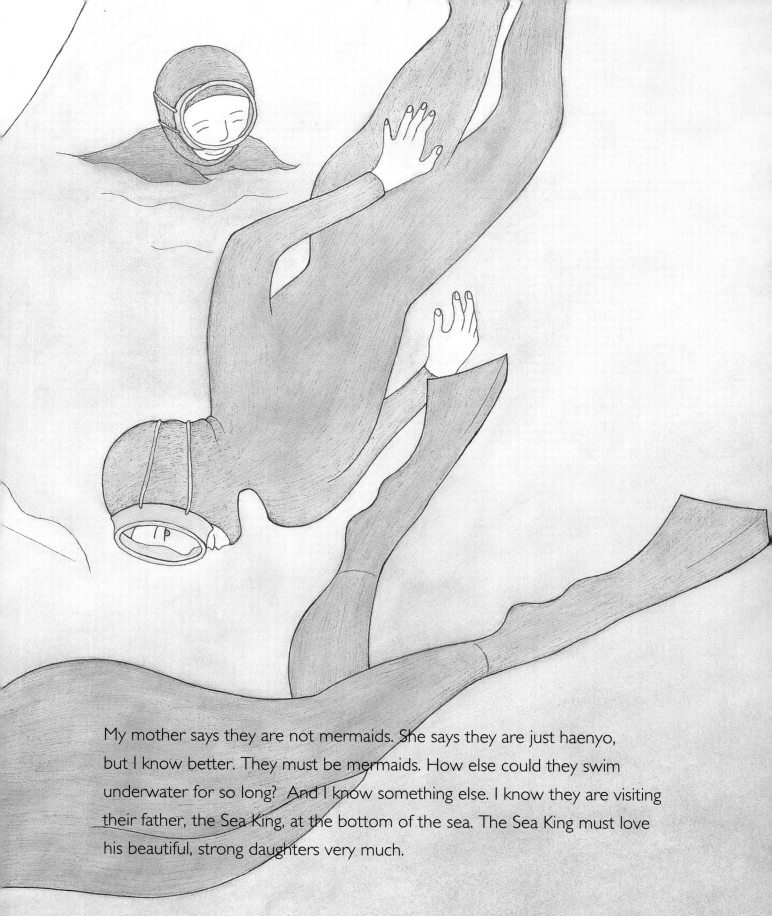

My mother says they are not mermaids. She says they are just haenyo, but I know better. They must be mermaids. How else could they swim underwater for so long? And I know something else. I know they are visiting their father, the Sea King, at the bottom of the sea. The Sea King must love his beautiful, strong daughters very much.

The bell rings and I am free. I run out to my bicycle.

My elder sister calls, "Come home with me. Stay away
from the beach!" But I don't listen. I ride away as fast as I can.

My sister does not want to be a mermaid. She wants
to wear nice clothes and listen to music and talk to boys.

My mother does not want me to be a mermaid. She says it is dangerous. She wants me to be a teacher or a doctor or a mother instead. I am not allowed at the beach. I should be doing my homework.

But I want to be a mermaid so every day I hide behind the black rocks and I watch and I listen so I will know how to grow. One day I will be a mermaid too.

I hear the waves crash. I smell the sea. I hear my mother and my grandmother and all their mermaid sisters singing in the waves.

Far out in the sea are a hundred mermaids. Their white drums float on the water. Their nets hang from the drums.

A head comes out of the water and a mermaid sings, "Sumbi-sori." It is a song that whistles, soft and high. It is the sigh of the mermaid leaving one home for another. For the haenyo, the mermaids, they walk on land too.

My grandmother is the oldest mermaid I know. She goes every day to the sea, to dive, to sing. She says it keeps her young. She says it keeps her alive.

I know the truth. The Sea King is her husband and she dives to visit him. She dives to keep him company and so she will not miss him.

I lie on the rocks. I look at the sky and watch the clouds. In school I learned that the clouds are water. That's when I discovered their secret. In the clouds I can watch the sea. I can look into the sky and watch the mermaids diving.

If I look very hard I can see Grandfather's castle standing tall
and bright in the clouds. I can see Grandfather's eyes. They
twinkle with laughter. One day I will visit him too.

The mermaids' song is over. I hear the mermaids talking. They come closer. They sound like a flock of seagulls, laughing, talking, shouting, laughing. They are so beautiful. They wear tight, black suits that show their bodies, slender and strong. They walk with straight backs, like queens. They laugh with white teeth and crinkled eyes.

I must run to my bicycle and ride quickly home. My mother must not see me here. They are close now. I waited too long. I look over the rocks and see my grandmother looking at me. She winks and walks away.

That night my grandmother reads me a story. It is the story of a mermaid who must choose to live on land or live in the sea.

"Why?" I ask my grandmother. "You live in the sea in the day and on land in the night."

"You are right," says my grandmother. "I am very fortunate. I can choose how to live."

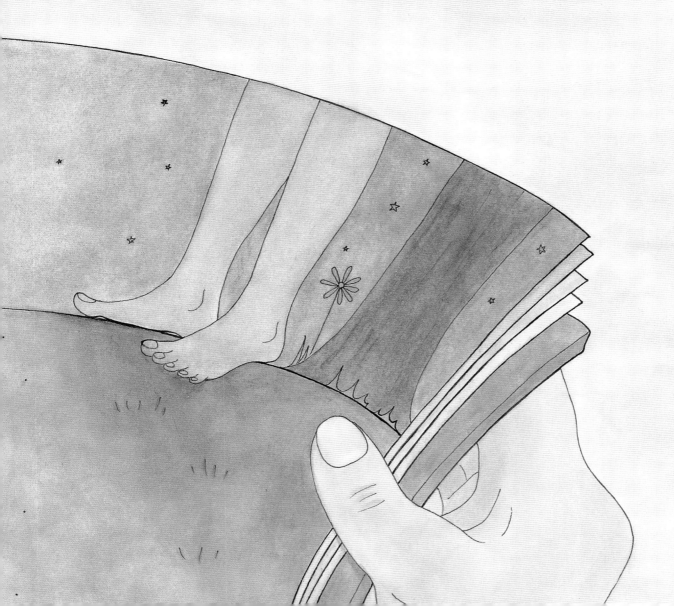

The next day I ride to the beach as fast as I can.
The wind is strong and it pushes me hard.
The clouds are dark and heavy.
I hear the waves crash on the shore.
I hear the mermaids singing.

I find my rock and I hide and watch. I see my mother's
head come up and hear her sing, "Sumbi-sori," and then
she disappears. There is my grandmother and then she is
gone. I watch for my mother. There she is.

My grandmother has not come back yet.
Maybe she is having tea with Grandfather.
I watch. Grandmother has been gone a
long time. "Sumbi-sori, sumbi-sori," sing
the mermaids. But something is wrong.
The song is changing. "Help! Help!" cry
the mermaids.

The mermaids are very far away, halfway to
their father's kingdom. No one is nearby.
Only I can hear them. "Help!" cries my
mother. "A jellyfish has stung Ae Sook!"

Grandmother! She was not having tea with Grandfather. She was in trouble. I am so afraid that I cannot move. Then I think of what Grandmother would do, of what my mother would do.

I run for my bicycle. There is a house on the hill above me. I ride as hard as I can. The man who lives there is a fisherman. I call for him. He comes running down the hill with me and we jump into his boat.

The mermaids are not singing. Where is my grandmother?

Mermaids surround the boat. The fisherman lifts one of them out of the water.

It is my grandmother. We wrap her in blankets and I cradle her head in my lap.

My mother climbs into the boat. "Jae Hyun, what are you doing here?"

"I brought the fisherman," I say. I am crying.

As the boat speeds away my mother puts her arm around me. She holds my grandmother's hand.

"Grandmother will be fine," she tells me.
"You saved her life."

"I was so afraid," I say.

"You were afraid but you saved her anyway," says
my mother. "That is true bravery. I am proud of you,
Jae Hyun. Today you acted like a haenyo."

My mother holds me tight but I still can't stop crying.

My grandmother is home again. She lies in bed and looks out her window at the sea.
I sit with her so she won't be lonely.

"Jae Hyun," says my grandmother, "you see that being a mermaid is dangerous. You
know you do not need to be one. You can go to school and become anything you want."

"Then I want to be a mermaid," I say.

My grandmother nods. "You are brave and you are strong. One day you will make a
very good mermaid." She looks up at my mother who stands in the doorway.
They look at each other a long time and then my mother bows her head
and turns to me.

"Come along," says my mother.

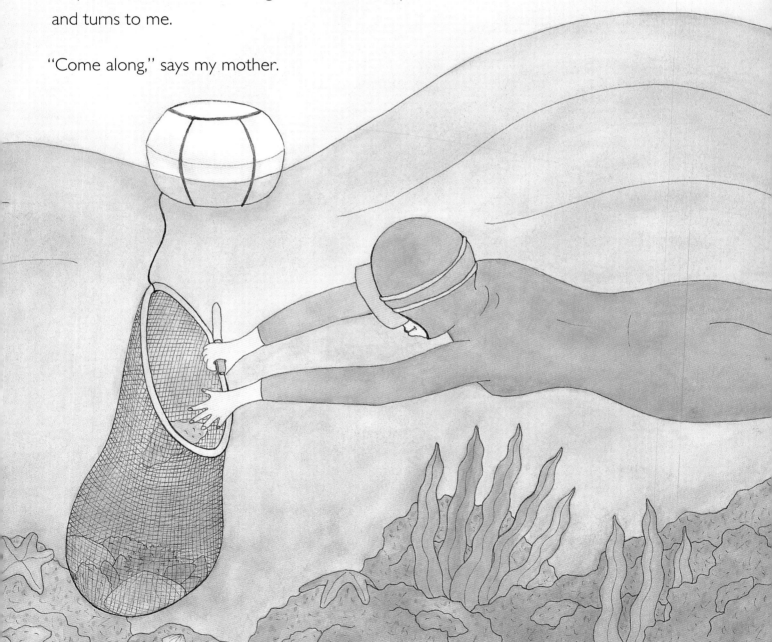

Grandmother waves from the window as I walk with my mother down the road.

"Where are we going?" I ask.

"To work," says my mother.

I do not understand what she means.

She squeezes my hand. "You may sit on the rocks and watch the haenyo. You may sit every day after school and learn. And one day, when I think you are ready, you may come in the sea with us."

I am going to be a mermaid. A haenyo. I am going to watch and learn and grow. I am going to sing with the mermaids and be strong with them. I will be brave with them and I will work hard. And, one day soon, I will visit my grandfather's kingdom under the sea.

AUTHOR'S NOTE

Jeju Island, in South Korea, is a volcanic island known for its black rock, its wind, and its women. The strong, independent women who dive for treasure on the ocean floor are called haenyo, which means "sea women." There have always been more women than men on Jeju Island and often there were not enough men to look after all the families. Hundreds of years ago women began diving on Jeju Island to support their families. Often their husbands stayed home to care for the children because wives could earn more money than their men could.

The haenyo dive for seaweed and shellfish and other creatures that live on the bottom of the ocean. They can dive as deep as twenty meters and can remain underwater for up to two minutes. The song of the haenyo, "sumbi-sori," is the whistling sound they make when they rise to the surface and expel the spent air in their lungs.

When they surface for air they rest by hanging on to a taewak, which is an empty gourd that floats on the water. The mangsari is a basket which hangs from the taewak and holds the shell openers, spades, and harpoons the haenyo use to do their work.

The haenyo have a very dangerous job. They are sometimes attacked by jellyfish and sharks and other ocean creatures. Many of them suffer from severe headaches from the intense water pressure they experience from diving so deep in the ocean.

Most of the women who dive today do so to provide a better life for their daughters, paying for their education so that they do not need to become haenyo themselves. In the 1950s there were as many as 30,000 haenyo on Jeju Island, but today there are fewer than 6000. More than half of them are over the age of seventy and none of them are under the age of thirty. It may not be long before the haenyo, the mermaids of Jeju, are just a memory.

For mermaids everywhere – Cynthia

To Seoha – Jumin

Published in 2011 by Simply Read Books www.simplyreadbooks.com

Text © 2011 Cynthia Heinrichs · Illustrations © 2011 Jumin Lee

Library and Archives Canada Cataloguing in Publication

Heinrichs, Cynthia

Mermaids / written by Cynthia Heinrichs ; illustrated by Jumin Lee.

ISBN 978-1-897476-37-6

I. Lee, Jumin II. Title.

PS8615.E365M47 2011   jC813'.6   C2010-905674-4

We gratefully acknowledge for their financial support of our publishing program the Canada Council for the Arts, the BC Arts Council, and the Government of Canada through the Book Publishing Industry Development Program (BPIDP).

Manufactured by Hung Hing in China, March 2011
This product conforms to CPSIA 2008

Book design by Leigh-Anne Mullock

10 9 8 7 6 5 4 3 2 1